Faraway Fox

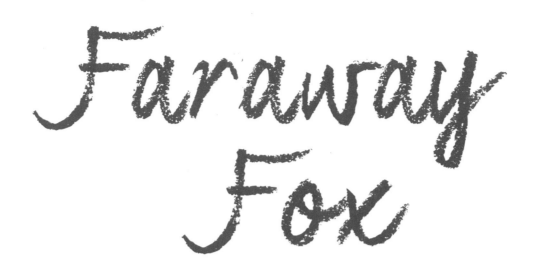

Written by
Jolene Thompson

Illustrated by
Justin K. Thompson

HOUGHTON MIFFLIN HARCOURT
Boston   New York

This was the forest where I lived with my family.

We used to race through the undergrowth and rest under the great shade trees after playing all day.

As kits, we spent our summer splashing in the stream and catching frogs while our parents went out to hunt.

My sister would always
catch the most.

I wonder where she is now?

And where's my big brother? We both loved the water and we'd have contests to see who could swim the fastest and the farthest.

My mother is a great hunter and taught me well.

She's so fast and so quiet, the prey never hears her coming.

I miss her advice.

I miss my father, too.

He and I once came across
a deer that had fallen into a
hole in the woods. It was too
deep to climb out.

The deer was trapped.

Like me.

I was separated from my family. Now my only company is these strange creatures. How do they stand on their hind legs for so long?

Why are these creatures digging?
I remember having to dig burrows
with my family.

It took a long time, so we would all take turns to make sure it was big enough for everyone.

This new burrow is . . . empty.

It's hard to believe . . .

Did they build this for me?

Could it be?

After all this time . . .

I am home!

Author's Note

The idea for this book was sparked when my youngest son asked why we encounter so many wild animals throughout our neighborhood and even in our own backyard. We talked about human encroachment into the habitats of wild animals, how so many of them end up trapped by human development, and the measures that are being taken to minimize our impact on the environment.

Around the world, people and governments are making an effort to improve conditions and safety for wildlife. Wildlife crossings including underpasses, overpasses, viaducts, tunnels, and more provide safe passage over and under roads and ensure that animals aren't cut off from valuable resources (and in Fox's case, family members!). These efforts make us safer as well, by helping to eliminate road collisions and dangerous interactions in urban environments. France was the first country to build wildlife crossings, while the Netherlands is the world leader with more than six hundred! In addition to foxes, animals big and small and as varied as coyotes, mountain lions, deer, salamanders, elephants, crabs, bears, turtles, and more have benefited from these efforts—even fish have been given special waterways. But there is a still a long way to go.

Unfortunately, there are not many wildlife crossing structures in the United States, even though a vehicle hits an animal *every twenty-six seconds* on U.S. highways. However, the California Department of Transportation, funded by an initial grant from the California Coastal Conservancy, along with the Santa Monica Mountains Conservancy, the Resource Conservation District of the Santa Monica Mountains, and the National Wildlife Federation, is working to create the biggest wildlife crossing in the world, over the U.S. 101 freeway in Southern California.

Below are just a few examples of some of the organizations that are working to improve life for humans and animals alike.

ARC-Animal Road Crossing www.arc-solutions.org
National Wildlife Federation www.nwf.org/How-to-Help/Garden-for-
    Wildlife.aspx
NWF Save LA Cougars www.savelacougars.org
Rocky Mountain Wild www.rockymountainwild.org/programs/wildlife-
    and-plants/habitat-connectivity
Montana's People's Way Partnership www.peopleswaywildlifecrossings.org
US DOT Federal Highway Administration www.fhwa.dot.gov/
    environment/wildlife_protection
Wildlife and Roads www.wildlifeandroads.org
National Park Service www.fws.gov/urban/index.php
The Humane Society www.humanesociety.org/animals/wild_neighbors/
    humane-backyard/humane-backyard.html
Parks Canada www.pc.gc.ca

*For my sons, Ethan and Fox, and my parents, Bonnie and Dana.
And for every person, young and old, who wants to make the world
a better place for every living thing. —J.T.*

*To all the creatures, great and small, and the people
who would love and protect them. —J.K.T.*

A wildlife bridge in the Netherlands.

A wildlife tunnel under a busy road in Canada.

Text copyright © 2016 by Jolene Thompson
Illustrations copyright © 2016 by Justin K. Thompson
Top photo: © https://beeldbank.rws.nl, Public Works / Joop van Houdt; Bottom photo: © Parks Canada

www.hmhco.com

The text of this book is set in Minion Pro.

Library of Congress Catalog Control Number 2015018847
ISBN 978-0-544-70711-5
Manufactured in Malaysia
TWP 10 9 8 7 6 5 4 3 2 1
4500594741